Xenophon

'The Sea, The Sea'

TRANSLATED BY REX WARNER

PENGUIN EPICS

PENGUIN BOOKS

Published by the Penguin Group
Penguin Books Ltd, 80 Strand, London WC2R 0RL, England
Penguin Group (USA) Inc., 375 Hudson Street, New York, New York 10014, USA
Penguin Group (Canada), 90 Eglinton Avenue East, Suite 700, Toronto, Ontario, Canada M4P 2Y3
(a division of Pearson Penguin Canada Inc.)
Penguin Ireland, 25 St Stephen's Green, Dublin 2, Ireland (a division of Penguin Books Ltd)
Penguin Group (Australia), 250 Camberwell Road, Camberwell, Victoria 3124, Australia
(a division of Pearson Australia Group Pty Ltd)
Penguin Books India Pvt Ltd, 11 Community Centre, Panchsheel Park, New Delhi – 110 017, India
Penguin Group (NZ), cnr Airborne and Rosedale Roads, Albany,
Auckland 1310, New Zealand (a division of Pearson New Zealand Ltd)
Penguin Books (South Africa) (Pty) Ltd, 24 Sturdee Avenue,
Rosebank, Johannesburg 2196, South Africa

Penguin Books Ltd, Registered Offices: 80 Strand, London WC2R 0RL, England

www.penguin.com

This translation of *The Persian Expedition* first published in Penguin Books 1975
This extract published in Penguin Books 2006

3

Translation copyright © Rex Warner, 1975
All rights reserved

The moral right of the translator has been asserted

Taken from the Penguin Classics edition of *The Persian Expedition*, translated by Rex Warner

Typeset by Rowland Phototypesetting Ltd, Bury St Edmunds, Suffolk
Printed in England by Clays Ltd, St Ives plc

ISBN-13: 978-0-141-02631-2
ISBN-10: 0-141-02631-6

Contents

Note

This extract is taken from Xenophon's *The Persian Expedition*, an extraordinary eyewitness account of the attempt of a Greek mercenary army – the Ten Thousand – to help Prince Cyrus overthrow his brother and take the Persian throne. Here the story begins with the Greek army betrayed by their Persian employers and trapped in a hostile land.

I

Xenophon takes the initiative

With their generals arrested and the captains and soldiers who had gone with them put to death, the Greeks were in an extremely awkward position. It occurred to them that they were near the King's capital and that around them on all sides were numbers of people and cities who were their enemies; no one was likely in the future to provide them with a chance of buying food. They were at least a thousand miles away from Greece; they had no guide to show them the way; they were shut in by impassable rivers which traversed their homeward journey; even the natives who had marched on the capital with Cyrus had turned against them, and they were left by themselves without a single cavalryman in their army, so that it was evident that, if they won a victory, they could not kill any of their enemies, and if they were defeated themselves none of them would be left alive. With all this to reflect upon they were in a state of deep despondency. Only a few tasted food that evening, and a few lit fires. Many of them did not parade by the arms that night, but took their rest just where each man happened to be, and could not sleep because of their misery and their longing for their home lands and parents and wives and children, which they thought that they would never see again. In this state of mind they all took their rest.

There was an Athenian in the army called Xenophon, who accompanied the expedition neither as a general nor a captain nor an ordinary soldier. Proxenus, who was an old friend of his, had sent for him from his home and promised to make him the friend of Cyrus whom, he said, he valued above his own country. When Xenophon had read Proxenus's letter he consulted Socrates the Athenian about the proposed expedition, and Socrates, suspecting that friendship with Cyrus might involve complaints at Athens (since Cyrus was thought to have been very active in helping the Spartans in their war with Athens), recommended Xenophon to go to Delphi and consult the god on the question of the expedition. Xenophon went there and asked Apollo the following question: 'To what God shall I pray and sacrifice in order that I may best and most honourably go on the journey I have in mind, and return home safe and successful?' Apollo's reply was that he should sacrifice to the appropriate gods, and when Xenophon got back to Athens he told Socrates the oracle's answer. When Socrates heard it he blamed him for not first asking whether it was better for him to go on the expedition or to stay at home; instead of that he had made his own decision that he ought to go, and then inquired how he might best make the journey. 'However,' he said, 'since this was the way you put your question, you must do what the god has told you.'

Xenophon then made the sacrifices which the god had ordered and set sail. He found Proxenus and Cyrus at Sardis just on the point of starting on the march into the interior and he was introduced to Cyrus. Proxenus was eager for him to stay with them and Cyrus too joined him in this, saying that as soon as the campaign was over he would send him back home immediately. The expedition was supposed to be against the Pisidians. Xenophon thus joined the army under a false impression, though this was not the fault of Proxenus, since neither he nor anyone else among the Greeks, except for Clearchus, knew that the expedition was marching against the King. However, when they got to Cilicia, it already seemed obvious to everyone that it was against the King that they were marching. All the same, though unwillingly and with apprehensions about the journey, most people continued on the march, not wanting to lose face in each other's eyes, and in the eyes of Cyrus. Xenophon was no different from the rest, and now in their difficult position he was as miserable as anyone else and could not get to sleep. However, he got a little sleep in the end and had a dream. He dreamed that there was a thunderstorm and that a thunderbolt fell on his father's house and then the whole house was on fire. He woke up immediately, feeling very frightened, and considered that in some respects the dream was a good one, because in the midst of his difficulties and dangers he had dreamed of a great light from Zeus; but in other respects he was alarmed by it, because the dream seemed to him to have come from Zeus in his character of the King and the fire had seemed to blaze all round him and this might mean that he would not be able to leave the King's country but would be shut in on all sides by one difficulty or

3

another. But what is really meant by having a dream like this can be seen from what happened after the dream.

This is what did happen. As soon as he woke up the first thing that came into his head was this: 'What am I lying here for? The night is passing and at dawn the enemy will probably be here. If we fall into the King's hands, there is nothing to prevent us from seeing the most terrible things happening, from suffering all kinds of tortures and from being put to death in ignominy. Yet so far from anybody bothering to take any steps for our defence, we are lying here as though we had a chance of enjoying a quiet time. What city, then, do I expect will produce the general to take the right steps? Am I waiting until I become a little older? I shall never be any older at all if I hand myself over to the enemy today.'

Then he stood up and first of all called together Proxenus's captains. When they had come together, he said: 'I personally, captains, cannot sleep any more than, I expect, you can, and I can no longer lie still when I think of the position we are in. For there is no doubt that the enemy only made open war on us when they thought that their plans were complete, but on our side there is now nobody who is thinking out counter measures whereby we can put up as good a fight as possible. Yet if we relax and fall into the King's power, what sort of treatment can we expect from him? He is the man who cut off and fixed to a stake the head and hand of his own brother, his own mother's son, even when he was dead. So what sort of treatment can we expect, we who have no blood relation to take our side, and who marched against him with the intention of

4

deposing him and making him a subject, and killing him if we could? Will he not go to all possible lengths in trying to inflict on us every conceivable misery and so make all men afraid of ever marching against him again? No, it is surely clear that we must do everything in our power to avoid falling into his hands.

'Now, personally, while the truce was in force, I could never stop feeling sorry for us and looking with envy on the King and those on his side. I considered what a large and splendid country they had, what inexhaustible supplies, what quantities of servants, of cattle and gold and clothing material; and then I thought on the other hand of our men's prospects – that we could only get a share of all these good things by paying for it (and I knew that there were not many left who had the money to do so), and that the oaths we had sworn prevented us from acquiring supplies in any other way except by paying for them. When I reckoned all this up, I sometimes used to feel more misgivings about the truce than I now do about the war. Now, however, they have put an end to the truce, and I think that the period of their arrogance and of our uneasy feelings is also ended. For now these good things lie in front of us as prizes for whichever side shows itself to be the better men; the gods are judges of the contest, and they will naturally be on our side, since it was our enemies who took their names in vain, while we, with many good things before our eyes, resolutely kept our hands off them because of the oaths we had sworn to the gods. So it seems to me that we can enter the contest with much more confidence than they can. Then we are physically better able than they are to endure cold and heat and hardship; our morale is, with the gods on our side, better than theirs; and if the gods grant us victory, as they did before, our enemies are easier to wound and kill than we are.

'Quite likely there are others who feel the same as I do. Well then, in heaven's name, let us not wait for other people to come to us and call upon us to do great deeds. Let us instead be the first to summon the rest to the path of honour. Show yourselves to be the bravest of all the captains, with more of a right to leadership than those who are our leaders at present. As for me, if you are willing to take the initiative like this, I am prepared to follow you, and if you appoint me to be your leader I do not ask to be excused because of my age. Indeed I think I am already sufficiently grown up to act in my own defence.'

This was what Xenophon said, and, after listening to him, all the captains urged him to be their leader – all except for a man there called Apollonides, who had a Boeotian accent. This Apollonides declared that it was nonsense to say that there was any chance of safety except by getting, if it was possible, the King's goodwill, and at the same time he started talking about all their difficulties. Xenophon, however, cut him short and spoke as follows: 'My dear good man, you are the sort of person who neither understands what he sees nor remembers what he hears. Yet you were there with all the rest when the King, after Cyrus's death and in his pride because of it, sent and demanded that we should surrender our arms; and then, when we, so far from surrendering them, made ready for battle and went and encamped by his army, he left no stone unturned – sending people to negotiate, begging for a truce, providing us with supplies – until he got his truce. But when our generals and captains went into a conference, just as you are recommending, and left their arms behind, relying on the truce, what happened? Are they not at this moment being beaten and tortured and insulted, and are not even able, poor devils, to die, though death, I imagine, is what they are longing for? With all this knowledge in your possession, do you actually maintain that those who recommend self-defence are talking nonsense, and tell us to go and make another attempt at getting the King's goodwill? Soldiers, my view is that we should not suffer this fellow in our society; we should take away his captaincy, put the baggage on his back and use him as an animal. Being a Greek, and being what he is, he brings shame not only on his own native place but on the whole of Greece.'

Then Agasias the Stymphalian broke in and said: 'This fellow has got nothing to do either with Boeotia or with Greece. I have observed that he has holes in both his ears, just like a Lydian.' This was actually the case, and so they drove him out.

The others went round the various detachments and where there was a general still alive they called for him, or, in cases where he was missing, for his deputy commander; where there was a captain still alive, they called for the captain. When they had all assembled they sat down in front of the place where the arms were kept. The generals and captains assembled; there were about a hundred all together, and the meeting took place at about midnight. Hieronymus of Elis, the oldest of Proxenus's captains, then began the proceedings and spoke as follows: 'Generals and captains, in view of our present position we decided to meet together ourselves and to invite you to join us, so that, if possible, we might come to some useful decision. I now call upon Xenophon to speak as he has already spoken to us.'

Xenophon accordingly spoke as follows: 'Here is one thing which we all know, namely, that the King and Tissaphernes have made prisoners of all those of us whom they could and are obviously planning, if they can manage it, to destroy the rest of us. Our part, as I see it, is to do everything possible to prevent our ever coming into the power of the natives – indeed to see rather that they are in our power. I should like to assure you of this point – that you who have assembled here in your present numbers are placed in an extraordinarily responsible position. All these soldiers of ours have their eyes on you, and if they see that you are downhearted they will all become cowards, while if you are yourselves clearly prepared to meet the enemy and if you call on the rest to do their part, you can be sure that they will follow you and try to be like you. It is right, too, I think, that you should show some superiority over them. After all you are generals, you are officers and captains. In peace time you got more pay and more respect than they did. Now, in war time, you ought to hold yourselves to be braver than the general mass of men, and to take decisions for the rest, and, if necessary, to be the first to do the hard work. I think that first of all you could do a great service to the army by appointing generals and captains as quickly as possible to take the places of those whom we have lost. For where there is no one in control nothing useful or distinguished can ever get done. This is roughly true of all departments of life, and entirely true where soldiering is concerned. Here it is discipline that makes one feel safe, while lack of discipline has destroyed many people before now.

'Then I think that, after you have appointed the required number of officers, if you were to call a meeting of the rest of the soldiers and put some heart into them, that would be just what the occasion demands. At the moment I expect you realize, just as I do, how dispirited they were in handing in their arms for the night and in going on guard. In that condition I cannot see how any use can be made of them, whether by night or by day. But there will be a great rise in their spirits if one can change the way they think, so that instead of having in their heads the one idea of "what is going to happen to me?" they may think "what action am I going to take?"

'You are well aware that it is not numbers or strength that bring the victories in war. No, it is when one side goes against the enemy with the gods' gift of a stronger morale that their adversaries, as a rule, cannot withstand them. I have noticed this point too, my friends, that in soldiering the people whose one aim is to keep alive usually find a wretched and dishonourable death, while the people who, realizing that death is the common lot of all men, make it their endeavour to die with honour, somehow seem more often to reach old age and to have a happier life when they are alive. These are facts which you too should realize (our situation demands it) and should show that you yourselves are brave men and should call on the rest to do likewise.'

So he ended his speech. Chirisophus spoke after him and said: 'Up to now, Xenophon, the only thing I knew about you was that I had heard you were an Athenian. Now I congratulate you on your speech and your actions, and I should like to see here as many people of your sort as possible. Then we should have the right spirit all through the army. And now,' he went on, 'let us not waste time, my friends. Let us go away, and let those who are short of officers choose new ones. When you have chosen them, come to the centre of the camp and bring along those whom you have elected. Then we will muster the rest of the soldiers there. Tolmides the herald had better come with us.'

With these words he got to his feet so as to show that there should be no delay, that what was necessary should be done at once. Afterwards the following were chosen as officers: Timasion, a Dardanian, to take the place of Clearchus, Xanthicles, an Achaean, to take Socrates' place, Cleanor, an Arcadian, to take Agias's place, Philesius, an Arcadian, to take that of Menon, and Xenophon, an Athenian, in the place of Proxenus.

2

The council of war

Dawn was just breaking when the new officers were chosen, and they came to the centre of the camp and decided to post sentries and call the soldiers to a meeting. When the rest of the army were assembled, Chirisophus stood up first and spoke as follows: 'Soldiers, our position is undoubtedly difficult. We have lost some very able generals and captains and soldiers, and in addition to that even Ariaeus' men, who used to be on our side, have turned traitor to us. All the same what we have to do is to surmount our difficulties like brave men, not to give in, but to try, if we can, to win honour and safety by victory. And if that is beyond us, then at least let us die with honour, and never, so long as we live, come into the power of our enemies. For if we do, we shall have to suffer, I imagine, the sort of fate which I pray the gods will bring upon our opponents.'

Next Cleanor of Orchomenus stood up and spoke as follows: 'You can see with your own eyes, soldiers, how perjured and godless the King is. You can see the treachery of Tissaphernes. He it was who said that he was a neighbour of Greece, and that he would attach the greatest importance to saving our lives. On this understanding he swore on oath to us in person, he in person gave us his right hand, and in person he deceived our generals and made prisoners of them, showing so little respect for Zeus, the guardian of hospitality, that he actually shared a meal with Clearchus and then used this very fact to entrap and destroy our officers. Then there is Ariaeus, whom we were prepared to make King, and with whom we exchanged guarantees that neither would betray the other; he too, showing no fear of the gods or respect for the memory of the dead Cyrus, though he was treated with the utmost distinction by Cyrus when he was alive, has now left us and joined with Cyrus's bitterest enemies, with whom he is attempting to injure us, who were Cyrus's friends. Well, I pray that the gods will give these men what they deserve. As for us, who see all this, we must never again be deceived by them, but must fight as hard as we can, and bear whatever is the will of heaven.'

After him Xenophon stood up. He had put on the best-looking uniform that he could, thinking that, if the gods granted victory, victory deserved the best-looking armour, or if he was to die, then it was right for him to put on his best clothes and be wearing them when he met his death. He began his speech as follows: 'Cleanor has spoken of the natives' perjury and treachery, and I feel sure that you agree with what he has said. If, then, we want to make friends with them again, we shall have to be very downhearted indeed, when we consider what happened to our generals, who, because they trusted in their good faith, put themselves into their hands. But if our purpose is to take our arms in our hands and to make them pay for what they have done and for the future to fight total war against them, then, with the help of heaven, we have many glorious hopes of safety.'

Just as he was saying this, someone sneezed, and, when the soldiers heard it, they all with one accord fell on their knees and worshipped the god who had given this sign. Xenophon went on: 'I think, soldiers, that, since an omen from Zeus the Saviour appeared just when we were speaking about safety, we ought to make a vow that we will give thank-offerings to the god for our safety in the place where we first reach friendly soil, and we should also vow to offer sacrifices to the other gods to the best of our ability. Whoever agrees with this, put up his hand.'

Then they all raised their hands, and afterwards they made their vows and sang the paean.

The claims of religion having been thus satisfied, Xenophon started again and spoke as follows: 'I was just saying that we had many glorious hopes of safety. First of all, we have kept our oaths to the gods, while our enemies have broken theirs, and in addition to this perjured themselves in transgressing the truce. This being so, it is reasonable to suppose that the gods will be against our enemies, but will fight on our side; and they are capable of quickly making even the strong weak, and of saving the weak easily, when such is their will, even if they are in the midst of danger. And next I shall remind you of the dangers which our fathers also have been through, so that you may realize that it is right for you to be brave men and that, with the help of the gods, the brave find safety even from the worst of difficulties. Remember how the Persians and their friends came

with an enormous army, thinking that they would wipe
Athens off the face of the earth; but the Athenians had
the courage to stand up to them by themselves, and they
defeated them. On that occasion they had made a vow
to Artemis that they would sacrifice to her a goat for
every one of their enemies whom they killed, but, since
they could not get hold of enough goats, they decided
to sacrifice five hundred every year, and they are still
sacrificing them today. Then, when Xerxes later on collected his innumerable army and came against Greece,
there was another occasion when your fathers defeated
the fathers of these people both on land and on sea. You
can find proof of all this in the trophies we have, but the
greatest piece of evidence of all is the freedom of the
cities in which you have been born and brought up. For
you worship no man as a master, but only the gods.
These were the men whose sons you are; and I shall
certainly not say that you dishonour your fathers. Not
many days ago you were in battle order against the
children of our old enemies, and, though they were
many times your number, you, with the help of the
gods, defeated them. And on that occasion you showed
yourselves brave men in order to get Cyrus a kingdom;
but now the fight is on for your own safety, and therefore
I am sure it is right to expect from you much greater
courage and a much greater will to victory. Then, too,
you ought also to feel much greater confidence against
the enemy. On the last occasion you had had no experience of them and you could see their prodigious
numbers, but all the same in the spirit of your fathers
you had the courage to set about them. Now, however,

when you know from experience that, even if they are many times your number, they are not anxious to face you, what reason have you to be afraid of them any longer? Do not imagine that we are any the worse off because the native troops who were previously in our ranks have now left us. They are even greater cowards than the natives whom we have beaten, and they made this clear by deserting us and fleeing to the other side. It is far better to see people who want to be the first to run away standing in one's enemy's army than in one's own ranks.

'If any of you feel disheartened because of the fact that we have no cavalry, while the enemy have great numbers of them, you must remember that ten thousand cavalry only amount to ten thousand men. No one has ever died in battle through being bitten or kicked by a horse; it is men who do whatever gets done in battle. And then we are on a much more solid foundation than cavalrymen, who are up in the air on horseback, and afraid not only of us but of falling off their horses: we, on the other hand, with our feet planted on the earth, can give much harder blows to those who attack us and are much more likely to hit what we aim at. There is only one way in which cavalry have an advantage over us, and that is that it is safer for them to run away than it is for us.

'You may, of course, be quite confident about the fighting but upset by the fact that Tissaphernes will no longer show you the way, nor will the King provide opportunities of buying food. If this is so, then consider whether it is better to have Tissaphernes to guide us, a man who is quite clearly working against us, or to have prisoners whom we shall order to show us the way and who will know that, if they make any mistakes which affect us, they will be mistakes that will also affect their own persons and their own lives. And on the question of supplies, is it better to buy in the markets which they provide, where we have to pay a lot to buy a little (and we have no longer even got the money), or is it better to beat them in battle and then take our supplies for ourselves, each man taking the quantity he feels like having?

'You may realize that these alternatives are the better ones, but still think that the rivers are an insuperable obstacle and regard yourselves as having been led properly into a trap by crossing them. If so, then I will ask you to consider whether the natives have not done here a very stupid thing. For all rivers, however impassable they may be at a distance from their springs, can be forded, and without so much as getting one's knees wet, if one follows them up towards their sources. And even if we cannot get across the rivers, even if no one comes forward to show us the way, even then we have no reason to get downhearted. We could not call the Mysians better men than we are, yet we know that they hold many large and prosperous cities in the King's country and against the King's will. We know that the same is true of the Pisidians, and we saw with our own eyes how the Lycaonians have seized the fortified positions in the plains and enjoy the profit of the land that belongs to these natives. Now in our case I should say that we ought not to make it obvious that we are setting off home, but we should make our dispositions as though we had the idea of settling here. I am certain that the King would offer the Mysians all the guides they wanted, and would give them numbers of hostages to guarantee his good faith in sending them out of the country and would actually build roads for them, even though they wanted to go away in four-horse chariots. And I am certain that he would be three times as pleased to do all this for us, if he saw that we were planning to stay here. No, what I am really afraid of is that, if we once learn to live a life of ease and luxury, enjoying the company of these fine great women, the wives and daughters of the Medes and Persians, we might be like the Lotus-eaters and forget about our road home. So I think that it is right and reasonable for us to make it our first endeavour to reach our own folk in Greece and to demonstrate to the Greeks that their poverty is of their own choosing, since they might see people who have a wretched life in their own countries grow rich by coming out here. Soldiers, I need not elaborate the point. It is obvious that all these good things come to the conquerors.

'I must, however, deal with these questions – how we can make our march as free from danger as possible, and how, if we have to fight, we can fight to the best advantage. The first suggestion I shall make to you is to set fire to all the waggons we have, so that we may not be led by our animals but may be able to march wherever the interest of the army dictates. Then we should set fire to our tents as well: they too cause difficulties in transport, and are no use either for fighting or for getting provisions. Then let us get rid of all inessentials in the rest of our equipment, only keeping what we have for the purpose of fighting and eating or drinking, so that as many of us as possible may carry arms and as few as possible carry baggage. When people are defeated, as you know, all their property changes hands; and if we win, we must look upon our enemies as if they were carrying baggage for us.

'It remains for me to mention what I think is the most important point of all. You can see what our enemies thought about it. They did not dare to make war on us until they had made prisoners of our generals, and this was because they thought that, so long as we had commanders and we were obedient to them, we were capable of coming out on top in the fighting; but once they had seized our commanders they thought that we would collapse through lack of control and lack of discipline. It is therefore necessary that the generals we have now should take much greater care than those we had before, and that those in the ranks should be much better disciplined and much more ready to obey their officers now than they were before. In cases of disobedience, we ought to vote that whichever of you happens to be on the spot should join with the officers in enforcing punishment. That would be the bitterest disappointment to our enemies; for, on the day that this is voted, they will see not one Clearchus but ten thousand, each one intolerant of any unsoldierly action.

'But it is time for me to make an end. It may be that the enemy will be upon us at once. If you agree with the suggestions I have made, then let us have them passed officially as soon as possible, so that they may be put into practice. If anyone knows a better way of going about things than the one I have outlined, then let him have the courage to tell us of it, even if he is only a common soldier. The safety which we are looking for is everyone's concern.'

Afterwards Chirisophus spoke. 'If we want,' he said, 'to pass any other measure in addition to those which Xenophon suggests, we can do so in a moment or two. I propose that, with no delay, we should vote that what he has just suggested is the best course to pursue. Will those who agree put up their hands?'

They all put their hands up, and Xenophon got up again and spoke as follows: 'Soldiers, listen to the additional proposals which I have to make. Obviously we must march somewhere where we can get provisions, and I gather that there are some fine villages not more than two miles away from here. But I should not be surprised if the enemy, like cowardly dogs that run after and try to bite anyone who goes past them, but run away from anyone who chases them – I should not be surprised if they too follow in our tracks as we go away. Perhaps then it would be safer for us to march with the hoplites forming a hollow square, so that the baggage and the general crowd may be more secure inside. If, then, we were told now who should be in the front of the square and organize the leading detachments, and who should be on the two flanks, and who should be responsible for the rear, we should not have to plan all this when the enemy are approaching us, but could immediately make use of those who have been specially detailed for the job. If anyone has a better suggestion to make, let us adopt it. If not, then I propose that Chiri-sophus should lead the square: he has the additional advantage of being a Spartan. Two generals, the oldest ones, should look after the two flanks; and the youngest of us, that is Timasion and myself, should be responsible for the rear. I suggest this as a temporary measure. Later on we shall have tried out this order of march, and we can decide on what seems best as different circumstances arise. If anyone has a better suggestion to make, I should like him to put it forward.'

Then, as nobody raised any objections, Xenophon said, 'Will those who agree with this put up their hands?' And the proposal was carried.

'Now then,' he continued, 'we must leave the meeting and put into operation what we have decided. Whoever wants to see his own people again must remember to be a brave soldier: that is the only way of doing it. Whoever wants to keep alive must aim at victory. It is the winners who do the killing and the losers who get killed. And those who want money must try to win battles. The winners can not only keep what they have themselves, but can take what belongs to the losers.'

3

The Greeks suffer from slings and arrows

At the conclusion of this speech they stood up and went away to set fire to their waggons and their tents. If anyone wanted any of the extra equipment, they shared it out among themselves and threw all the rest into the fire. When this was done, they had breakfast, and, while they were in the middle of it, Mithridates arrived with about thirty horsemen. He asked the generals to come within hearing and then spoke as follows: 'I, my Greek friends, was, as you know, faithful to Cyrus, and I am still a friend of yours. Also I find my present position here very alarming. If, then, I found that you were thinking of any safe way out, I should like to join you and bring all my followers with me. Tell me, then, what you propose to do, and consider me as a friend who is on your side and who would like to join you in your march.'

After a discussion the generals decided to give him the following reply. Chirisophus was the spokesman. 'What we have decided,' he said, 'is this: if we are allowed to make our way home, we shall go through the country doing as little damage as possible; but if anyone tries to stop us on our way, we shall fight our way out as hard as we can.'

Mithridates then made an attempt at proving that it

was impossible to get to safety against the King's will, and at this point he was recognized as having been sent with a hidden object in view. Indeed there was actually one of Tissaphernes' men in his company to ensure his reliability.

After this incident the generals decided that it would be better to make a resolution that, so long as they were in enemy country, the war should be conducted without any negotiations with the enemy, since ambassadors from the other side tended to seduce the soldiers' allegiance. They actually did seduce one of the captains, Nicarchus the Arcadian, who deserted in the night with about twenty men.

Next, after having had a meal, they crossed the river Zapatas and marched in battle order, with the baggage animals and the camp followers inside the square. Before they had gone far Mithridates again put in an appearance with about two hundred cavalry and about four hundred archers and slingers. These were lightly armed and very quick on their feet.

Mithridates approached the Greeks as though he was on friendly terms with them, but, as soon as they got close together, his men, both cavalry and foot, suddenly shot their arrows, while the others slung stones and caused some casualties. The Greek rearguard suffered badly, but were unable to retaliate, since their Cretan archers could not shoot so far as the Persians and also, being light troops, had taken refuge in the centre of the square; as for the javelin-throwers, their range was not great enough to reach the Persian slingers.

Xenophon then came to the conclusion that they

should drive the enemy back, and this was done by the hoplites and peltasts who were with him in the rearguard. In the pursuit, however, they failed to catch a single one of the enemy. This was because the Greeks had no cavalry, and their infantry could not, over a short distance, catch up with the enemy infantry, who ran away when they were still some way off. It was naturally impossible to press the pursuit over a long distance from the rest of the army. The native cavalry, however, by shooting backwards from on horseback, managed to inflict wounds even when they were in flight; and when the Greeks had pursued them for a certain distance, they had to fall back again over the same distance, fighting all the way. The result was that in the whole day they covered no more than two and a half miles. However, they reached the villages in the afternoon.

Here again there was much despondency. Chirisophus and the oldest of the generals blamed Xenophon for carrying on a pursuit away from the main body, and, in spite of the risks he ran, not being able to do any damage to the enemy. Xenophon listened to their criticism and admitted that they were right in blaming him, and had the facts on their side to prove their case. 'Nevertheless,' he said, 'I had to drive them back, when I saw that we were suffering badly by staying where we were and that we could do nothing in retaliation. Once we started driving them back, what you say is true. We were no better able to do them any damage, and we had the greatest difficulty in getting back ourselves. We should be grateful to the gods, then, that they did not come with a large force, but only in small numbers, with the result that, without doing us very great harm, they have shown us where we are deficient. At present the enemy archers can shoot further than our Cretans can shoot in reply, and their slingers can operate out of range of our javelin-throwers. When we drive them back, it is not possible for us to pursue them over much of a distance from the main army, and in a short distance no infantry-man, however fast he runs, can catch up with another infantryman who has a bow-shot's start of him. There-fore, if we are going to prevent them from having the power to harm us on the march, we must get hold of slingers and cavalry as soon as we can. There are some Rhodians, I hear, in our army, and they say that most of them know how to use a sling. Their weapon, too, has actually twice the range of the Persian sling. Persian slings do not carry far because they use stones as big as one's fist for throwing; but the Rhodians know how to use leaden bullets as well. If, then, we find out who has a sling in his possession, and pay for any there are, and pay more money to anyone who volunteers to make more slings, and think of some extra privilege we can give to anyone who volunteers to serve as a slinger in the ranks, then perhaps enough will come forward to be of use to us. I have noticed, too, that we have horses in the army: some are mine, others are part of Clearchus's property which he has left, and there are many more which we have captured and now use for carrying bag-gage. If, then, we sort them out, putting baggage animals in the place of some, and equipping horses for the use of cavalrymen, they too, perhaps, will give the enemy trouble when he runs away.'

This was agreed upon, and about two hundred slingers came forward that night. On the next day about fifty horses and cavalrymen were passed fit for service. They were provided with leather jerkins and breastplates, and Lycius the son of Polystratus, an Athenian, was given the command of the cavalry.

4

Tissaphernes still in pursuit

They halted for that day and went forward on the next, rising earlier than usual, as they had a watercourse to cross and were afraid that the enemy might attack them while they were crossing it. They had got across this before Mithridates again put in an appearance, this time with a thousand cavalry and about four thousand archers and slingers. He had asked and obtained this number of troops from Tissaphernes and had promised that if he got them, he would hand the Greeks over to him as prisoners. His low opinion of the Greeks was based on the fact that in the earlier attack he had come to no harm, in spite of his small numbers, and thought that he had inflicted severe losses on the Greeks.

When the Greeks were nearly a mile away from their crossing of the watercourse, Mithridates with his whole force moved over too. Orders had been issued to the necessary numbers of peltasts and hoplites to drive the enemy back, and the cavalry had been told to press the pursuit confidently, as adequate forces would be there to support them. When Mithridates caught them up and the sling-stones and arrows began to arrive, a trumpet was sounded, and immediately those who had been ordered to do so ran forward in a body and the cavalry made their charge. The enemy did not wait for them, but fled back to the watercourse. Many of the native infantry were killed in this pursuit and about eighteen of their cavalry were taken alive in the watercourse. The Greeks, acting on their own initiative, mutilated the corpses, so that the sight of them might cause as much fear as possible among the enemy.

After suffering this defeat the enemy retired, and the Greeks marched on safely for the rest of the day and reached the river Tigris. There was a large deserted city there called Larissa, which in the old days used to be inhabited by the Medes. It had walls twenty-five feet broad and a hundred feet high, with a perimeter of six miles. It was built of bricks made of clay, with a stone base of twenty feet underneath. At the time when the Persians seized the empire from the Medes, the King of the Persians laid siege to this city but was quite unable to take it. A cloud, however, covered up the sun and hid it from sight until the inhabitants deserted the place, and so the city was taken. Near the city there was a pyramid of stone, a hundred feet broad, and two hundred feet high. Many of the natives from the neighbouring villages had run away and taken refuge on it.

From here a day's march of eighteen miles brought them to a large undefended fortification near a city called Mespila, which was once inhabited by the Medes. The base of this fortification was made of polished stone in which there were many shells. It was fifty feet broad and fifty feet high. On top of it was built a brick wall fifty feet in breadth and a hundred feet high. The perimeter of the fortification was eighteen miles. Medea, the King's wife, is supposed to have taken refuge here at the time when the Medes lost their empire to the Persians, and the King of the Persians, when he besieged the city, could not take it either by the passing of time or by assault. Zeus, however, drove the inhabitants out of their wits with a thunderstorm, and so the city was taken.

Next came a day's march of twelve miles in the course of which Tissaphernes made his appearance. He had with him not only his own cavalry, but also the force which Orontas (the man who had married the King's daughter) commanded, the native troops which Cyrus had commanded on his march inland, the troops with which the King's brother had come to reinforce the King, and, in addition, all the troops which the King had given him; so that his army appeared enormous. On coming close, he brought up some of his companies to the rear of the Greeks, and led others round on the flanks, but did not dare to make a direct assault or show any willingness to take a risk. Instead he ordered his men to use their slings and bows. Then the Rhodians, who were posted at intervals in the Greek ranks, used their slings, and the archers shot their arrows, and no one failed to hit a man (indeed one could hardly miss if one tried to), and Tissaphernes got out of range with alacrity, as did the rest of his army.

For the remainder of the day the Greeks marched on, with the Persians following them. The natives did no further damage by their old methods of long-range fighting since the Rhodians could sling further than the Persian slingers and further even than most of their archers. The Persians use large bows, and so all the arrows of theirs which were picked up came in useful to the Cretans, who constantly used the enemy's arrows and practised long-range shooting with a high trajectory. A number of bow-strings were found in the villages, and some lead also which could be used for the slings.

On that day, then, after the Greeks had come to some villages and encamped, the natives retired, having had the worst of the long-range fighting. Next day the Greeks stayed where they were and provided themselves with food, of which there was a good supply in the villages. On the day after that they continued their march over the plain, with Tissaphernes following them and shooting at them from a distance. On this march the Greeks came to the conclusion that the square was a bad formation to adopt when the enemy were in the rear. When the two flanks of the square are compressed, because of the road becoming narrower, or in going through a pass in the mountains or in crossing a bridge, what is bound to happen is that the hoplites get pushed out of position and make heavy going of it, crowded together as they are, and confused; and the result is that, when they are in this disordered state, one can make no use of them. Then, when the flanks diverge again, those who were previously pushed out of position are bound to get dispersed, and the space between the two flanks is not filled up, and, when this happens to the men they get dispirited with the enemy at their heels. So whenever they had to make any sort of crossing, over a bridge or anything else, each man struggled to be the first across, and that gave the enemy an excellent chance of attacking them.

The generals took note of this situation, and formed

six companies of a hundred men each. They appointed captains for the companies and other commanders for each fifty men and for each twenty-five men. Whenever the two flanks were pushed in on each other on the march, these six companies waited behind, so as not to cause any disorder in the flanks: afterwards they came up again on the left and right of the flanks. And when the sides of the square opened out, they would fill up the centre, marching into the opening, if it was a small one by companies with six men in front, or if it was larger with twelve men in front, or if it was very large indeed with twenty-five men in front, so that the centre of the square was always full. When they had to make any crossing, by a bridge or otherwise, they preserved their order, the captains leading their companies across in turn. They were also ready for action if there was any demand for it in any part of the main body.

In this formation they went forward for four days. In the course of the fifth day's march they noticed a kind of palace with a number of villages in its neighbourhood, and saw that the road to the palace went across high ground which formed the foothills of the mountain beneath which the village was. The Greeks were pleased to see the hills, as was natural enough considering that their enemy's force was of cavalry; but when they had marched on and, after ascending the first hill, had just gone down into the valley to ascend the next, the natives made an attack on them. Whipped on to it under the lash, they hurled their javelins and sling-stones and arrows from their high ground down on to the ground below, inflicting a number of wounds. They got the upper hand of the Greek light troops and kept them penned up inside the square of hoplites, so that for that day both the slingers and the archers, being mixed up with the general crowd, were of no use at all. When the Greeks tried to escape from their difficulties by driving the enemy back, they, being hoplites, found it hard going to get to the top of the hill, while the enemy darted away from them quickly. Again, when they made their way back to the rest of the army, they suffered just as before, and the same thing happened on the second hill. They therefore decided not to allow the soldiers to move from the third hill until they had led up into the mountain a force of peltasts from the right flank of the square. When these peltasts got on to higher ground than the enemy who were coming after, the enemy gave up attacking the troops on their descent, since they were frightened of being cut off and having enemies on both sides of them. They marched in this way for the rest of the day, some by the road over the hills and others keeping pace with them along the mountain, until they came to the villages. They then appointed eight doctors, as there were a number of wounded.

They stayed here for three days, partly for the sake of the wounded, and partly because they could get plenty of food – wheat-flour and wine and a lot of barley that had been stored there for horses. All this had been collected for the man who was satrap of the country.

On the fourth day they went down to the plain; but when Tissaphernes and his force caught them up, they took the lesson of hard facts which was to encamp at the first place where they saw a village and not to go on marching and fighting at the same time. This was because they had many men out of action, both the wounded and those who were bearing them, and those who took over the arms of the bearers. However, when they had encamped and the natives advanced on the village in an attempt to engage in long-range fighting, the Greeks had very much the better of it. There was a great difference between starting from one's own ground to repel the enemy, and fighting while on the march with the enemy at one's heels.

In the middle of the afternoon came the time for the enemy to retire, as the natives (fearing that the Greeks might make a night attack) always encamped at least six miles away from the Greek army. A Persian army is useless at night, since their horses are tethered and usually tied by the feet as well, so that they cannot run away if they are loosed. If, then, there is a disturbance, the horses have to be caparisoned for their Persian riders, and bridled, and then the rider has to put on his armour and mount – all of which is difficult to do by night and in the middle of an uproar. This was the reason why they camped a great distance away from the Greeks.

Now, when the Greeks became aware that the enemy wanted to retire and indeed were passing round the order to do so, they issued, in the enemy's hearing, an order to their own troops that they should get their baggage together. The natives then put off their departure for a time, but when it got late they went off, not thinking it desirable to march and come into camp by night.

The Greeks, seeing that they were now undoubtedly

retiring, broke camp themselves and marched away, doing as much as six miles. This put such a distance between the two armies that there was no sign of the enemy either on the next day or on the day after that. On the fourth day the natives, who had gone forward during the night, occupied a commanding position on the right of the road by which the Greeks intended to march. This was one of the heights of a mountain which overlooked the way down into the plain. When Chirisophus saw that this height had been occupied in advance of them he summoned Xenophon from the rear and asked him to bring his peltasts and come to the front. Xenophon, however, observed Tissaphernes and his whole force coming into sight and so he did not lead the peltasts forward. Instead he rode up himself to Chirisophus and asked him, 'Why are you calling for me?'

Chirisophus replied: 'You can see for yourself. The hill that overlooks our way down has been occupied in advance of us. We cannot get past unless we drive them off it. But why didn't you bring the peltasts?'

Xenophon replied that he did not think it was wise to leave the rear unguarded while the enemy were in sight. 'However,' he said, 'the time has certainly come to decide how one can dislodge those people from the hill.'

At this point Xenophon noticed that the summit of the mountain was higher than the ground on which their own army was and that there was a possible approach from it to the hill where the enemy were. So he said: 'The best thing to do, Chirisophus, is for us to advance on the summit as fast as we can. If we can occupy it, those who are commanding our road will not be able to maintain their position. If you like, you stay here with the main body. I will volunteer to go ahead. Or, if you prefer it, you march on the mountain and I will stay here.'

'I will give you the choice,' said Chirisophus, 'of doing whichever you like.'

Xenophon, pointing out that he was the younger man, chose to make the advance on the mountain, but asked Chirisophus to let him have some men from the front to go with him, as it would take time to bring up men from the rear. Chirisophus let him have the peltasts who were at the front and took those who were in the middle of the square. He also ordered the three hundred, all picked men, whom he had under his personal command at the front of the square to go with Xenophon.

They then marched away as quickly as they could, but when the enemy on the hill saw that the Greeks were making their way to the summit, they too started off immediately to contest the position. Then there was a lot of shouting, from the Greek army cheering on its men on the one side and from Tissaphernes's people cheering on their men on the other side. Xenophon rode along the ranks on horseback, urging them on. 'Soldiers,' he said, 'consider that it is for Greece you are fighting now, that now you are fighting your way to your children and your wives, and that with a little hard work now, we shall go on the rest of our way unopposed.'

Soteridas, a man from Sicyon, said: 'We are not on a level, Xenophon. You are riding on horseback, while I am wearing myself out with a shield to carry.'

When Xenophon heard this, he jumped down from

his horse, pushed Soteridas out of the ranks, took his shield away from him and went forward on foot as fast as he could, carrying the shield. He happened to be wearing a cavalry breastplate as well, so that it was heavy going for him. He kept on encouraging those in front to keep going and those behind to join up with them, though struggling along behind them himself. The other soldiers, however, struck Soteridas and threw stones at him and cursed him until they forced him to take back his shield and continue marching. Xenophon then remounted and, so long as the going was good, led the way on horseback. When it became impossible to ride, he left his horse behind and hurried ahead on foot. And so they got to the summit before the enemy.

5

Between the Tigris and the mountains

The natives thereupon turned tail and fled in all directions, and the Greeks held the summit. The army with Tissaphernes and Ariaeus turned aside, and went off by another way, and Chirisophus's men descended into the plain and camped in a village that was full of good things. In this plain beside the Tigris there were a number of other villages too, equally well provided.

However, in the late afternoon the enemy suddenly appeared in the plain and cut off some of the Greeks who were scattered about there and were engaged in plunder, as several herds of cattle had been caught as they were being taken across to the other side of the river. Tissaphernes and his men then tried to set fire to the villages, and there were some of the Greeks who became very downhearted about this, since they got the idea that, if they burned the villages, they would have nowhere to get supplies from.

Chirisophus and his men had just returned from rescuing those in the plain, and Xenophon, who was met by the rescue party when he came down from the hill, rode along their ranks and said: 'Do you see, Greeks, that they are admitting that we are now the owners of their land? When they were arranging the truce they made a great point of this, that there should be no burning of the King's land; and now they are burning it themselves as though it wasn't his. But if they have any food for themselves anywhere, they will see us marching there too. Really, Chirisophus, I think we ought to consider this property our own and stop them burning it.'

Chirisophus said: 'I don't think so. But we might help them in the job, and then they will stop all the sooner.'

When they got back to their quarters the generals and captains had a meeting, while the rest were occupied with the provisions. They were now in a very difficult position. On one side there were mountains of a very great height and on the other side was the river, which was so deep that when they tested the depth, not even the spears stood out above the water. While the generals were uncertain what to do, a man from Rhodes came forward and said: 'I will undertake to bring you across in parties of four thousand hoplites at a time, if you will supply me with what I need and give me a talent by way of payment.'

When they asked him what he needed, he said: 'I shall need two thousand bags made of hide, and I can see that there are numbers of sheep and goats and oxen and asses about. When we have skinned them and inflated their hides they will give us an easy means of getting across. I shall also need the ropes which you use for the baggage animals. With these ropes I shall tie the bags together and keep each bag in its place by fastening stones to it and letting them down into the water like anchors. Then I shall string the bags across the river and fasten them to both banks; then put wood on top of them and cover the wood with earth. I can make it clear to you in a moment that there is no risk of sinking. Each bag will keep two men from sinking; and the wood and earth will stop them slipping off.'

The generals listened to him, but thought that, though it was a nice idea, it was impossible to put into practice, as there were great numbers of cavalry on the further bank to stop them getting over, and they would immediately have prevented the first people across from doing their jobs.

Next day they went back again over their former route to the villages that had not been burned. They set fire to the villages from which they started, so that the enemy did not come close to them, but watched them from a distance, wondering, apparently, where the Greeks would go next and what their intentions were. The generals then held another meeting, while the rest of the army was occupied with provisions. They brought in the prisoners and questioned them in detail about the country all round them. The replies were to the effect that the country to the south was on the road to Babylon and Media, the way, indeed, by which they had come; the way eastward led to Susa and Ecbatana, which was said to be the King's summer residence; if one crossed the river and went westward the way went to Lydia and Ionia; and the road going north over the mountains led to the Carduchi. These people, they said, lived in the mountains and were very warlike and not subject to the King. Indeed a royal army of a hundred and twenty thousand had once invaded their country, and not a man of them had got back, because of the terrible conditions of the ground they had to go through. However, on occasions when they made a treaty with the satrap who controlled the plain there was mutual intercourse between the Carduchi and them.

The generals listened to these reports and separated out those who said they knew the road in each direction, not giving any indication of which one they were going to take. They thought, however, that they would have to invade the country of the Carduchi across the mountains, since according to the prisoners, once they had got through these people, they would arrive in Armenia, a big rich country governed by Orontas; and from there, the prisoners said, it was easy going in whatever direction one wished to march.

They held sacrifices to bless this project, so that they could start the march when they thought the right time had come. As it was, they feared that the pass over the mountains might be occupied in advance of them. Then they issued orders that, after supper, everyone should pack up his belongings and rest: they should be ready to follow their officers at the word of command.

6

The entry into Kurdestan

At about the last watch, with enough of the night remaining for them to be able to cross the plain under cover of darkness, they got up when the signal was given and marched toward the mountain, which they reached at dawn. Chirisophus then took the lead with his own troops and also all the light troops; Xenophon brought up the rear with the hoplites of the rearguard, but with no light troops at all, as there seemed to be no danger of any attack being made on them from the rear while they were on the ascent.

Chirisophus reached the summit before any of the enemy realized what was happening. He then went steadily forward, and as the various contingents of the army crossed the pass they followed him into the villages which lay in the folds and recesses of the mountains. The Carduchi immediately abandoned their houses and fled into the mountains with their women and children. Plenty of food remained for the Greeks to take, and there were a lot of brazen utensils in the furniture of the houses too. The Greeks did not take any of these, or pursue the people. They wished to behave leniently on the chance that the Carduchi, since they were enemies of the King, might be willing for them to go through their country peaceably. Food, however, was a matter of necessity, and they took whatever they came across. The Carduchi paid no attention when they called out to them, and indeed gave no signs at all of friendly feeling.

It was already dark when the last of the Greeks had come down from the summit to the villages, since, owing to the narrowness of the road, the ascent and descent had taken up the whole day. At this point some of the Carduchi got together in a body and made an attack on the last of the Greeks. They killed some and wounded others with stones and arrows, though they were not in great numbers, as the Greek army had come upon them unexpectedly. Indeed, if more of them had got together on this occasion, a large part of the army might possibly have been wiped out.

So for that night they encamped as they were in the villages, and the Carduchi lit a number of beacons on the mountains all round them as signals to each other. At dawn it was decided at a meeting of the Greek generals and captains to take on the march only the strongest and most essential of the baggage animals, and to leave the rest behind; also to let go all the slaves in the army that had been captured recently. This was because the great number of baggage animals and slaves slowed up the march, and there were numbers of men who were in charge of these and so were out of action; and with so many people on the march, they had to provide and transport double the necessary quantity of supplies. After having made this decision, they gave orders by herald that it was to be carried into effect.

When they had had breakfast and started on their

way, the generals stationed themselves in a narrow part of the road and took away from the soldiers any of the proscribed articles which they found had not been left behind. The men did as they were told, though there were some cases of people getting away with things, cases when a soldier was in love with a particularly good-looking boy or woman. For that day, then, they went ahead, having a certain amount of fighting to do and resting from time to time.

On the next day there was a great storm, but they had to go forward as there were not sufficient supplies. Chirisophus was leading the march and Xenophon was with the rearguard. The enemy made violent attacks and in the narrow passes came to close range with their bows and slings with the result that they had to travel slowly, as they were constantly chasing the enemy off and then returning again. Xenophon had often to order a halt when the enemy launched his violent attacks; and on these occasions Chirisophus, when the word was passed forward, halted his men too; but on one occasion he did not stop, but led on fast, passing back the word to follow him. It was obvious that something was the matter, but there was no time to go forward and see what was the cause of this haste. The result was that for the rearguard the march almost turned into a full retreat. Here a gallant Spartan soldier, called Leonymus, was killed by an arrow which went into the side of his body through the shield and the jerkin, and Basias the Arcadian was also killed, shot clean through the head.

When they reached the place where they were to camp, Xenophon went just as he was to Chirisophus and blamed him for not waiting, the result of which had been that the soldiers had had to fight at the same time as they were retreating. 'And now,' he said, 'two most gallant fellows have been killed, and we could not recover their bodies or bury them.'

Chirisophus replied: 'Look at the mountains. See how impassable they are in every direction. This one road, which you see, is a steep one, and you can see that there are men on it, a great crowd, who have occupied the pass and are on guard there. That is why I was in a hurry and so did not wait for you. I thought there was a chance of being able to get there first, before the pass was seized. The guides we have say that there is no other road.'

Xenophon said: 'I have got two men. When the enemy were giving us trouble, we set an ambush – which also gave us a chance of getting our breath back – and we killed some of them, and made up our minds to take a few alive just for this very reason, to have the services of guides who know the country.'

At once they brought the two men and questioned them separately, to see if they knew of any other road apart from the obvious one. One of the two, although he was threatened in every kind of way, said that he did not know of any other road. Since he said nothing that was of any help he was killed, with the other man looking on. The survivor then said that the reason why the other man had denied knowledge of another road was that he happened to have a daughter who had been married to somebody in that direction. He declared that he would lead them by a road that was a possible one for animals as well as men. He was then asked whether there was any part of the road which was difficult to get past, and he replied that there was one height which it would be impossible to pass, unless it was occupied in advance. It was then decided to call a meeting of the captains, peltasts and hoplites as well, to give them an account of the situation, and ask who was willing to do a good job and come forward as a volunteer for the expedition. The hoplites who came forward were Aristonymus the Methydrian and Agasias the Stymphalian, and Callimachus of Parrhasia put forward a separate claim for himself, saying that he was willing to go, if he could take with him volunteers from the whole army. 'Personally,' he said, 'I am sure that a lot of the young men will follow if I am their leader.' Then they asked if any of the officers of the light-armed troops would volunteer to join with the others. Aristeas of Chios came forward, a man who, on many occasions of this sort, was worth a lot to the army.

7

Fighting in the mountains

It was now afternoon, and they told the volunteers to
have their food and then start. They bound the guide
and handed him over to them, and made arrangements
that, if they took the height, they should guard the
position for the night and give a trumpet signal at dawn:
those on the height should then make an attack on the
Carduchi holding the regular way out of the valley, while
the rest of them should proceed as quickly as they could
and join up with them.

After agreeing on this plan, the volunteers set out, a
force of about two thousand. There was a lot of rain at
the time. Xenophon, with the rearguard, led on towards
the regular exit from the valley, in order that the enemy
might give their attention to this part of the road and
that the party which was making a detour might, as
far as possible, escape detection. However, when the
rearguard got to a watercourse which they had to cross
to make their way up to the higher ground, the natives
at this point rolled down boulders big enough to fill a
waggon, some bigger, some smaller, which came crash-
ing down against the rocks and ricocheted off, so that
it was absolutely impossible even to get near the pass.
Some of the captains, finding things impossible in one

direction, tried somewhere else, and continued their efforts until it became dark. Then, when they thought that their retreat would be unobserved, they went back for supper. Those of them who had been in the rearguard had not had any breakfast either. The enemy, however, went on rolling down stones all through the night, as was evident from the noise.

Meanwhile the men who had taken the guide went round in a detour and came upon the guards sitting round their camp fire. They killed some of them and drove the others downhill, and then stayed there under the impression that they were occupying the height. This, however, was not the case. Above them there was a small hill, past which ran the narrow road where the guard had been stationed. Nevertheless there was a way from this position to where the enemy was stationed on the regular road.

They passed the night where they were, and, at the first sign of dawn, formed up and marched in silence against the enemy. As there was a mist they got close up to them without being noticed. Then, as soon as they came into sight of each other, the trumpet sounded, and they raised their war-cry and charged down on the men, who did not wait for them, but abandoned the road and fled. Only a few were killed, as they were quick on their feet.

Meanwhile Chirisophus's men, on hearing the trumpet, immediately attacked uphill along the regular road; and some of the generals advanced along little-used paths, just where they happened to find themselves, climbing up as best they could and pulling each other up with their spears. These were the first ones to join up with that party that had previously occupied the position.

Xenophon, with half the rearguard, went by the same way as those who had the guide, as it was the easiest going for the baggage animals. He had placed the other half of his men in the rear of the animals. As they went forward they came to a ridge commanding the road and found it occupied by the enemy. They had either to dislodge them or else be cut off from the rest of the Greeks. They themselves might have gone by the same road as the others, but this was the only possible route for the baggage animals. Then they shouted out words of encouragement to each other and made an assault on the ridge with the companies in column. They did not attack from every direction but left the enemy a way of escape, if he wanted to run away. So long as they were climbing up, each man by the best route he could find, the natives shot arrows at them and hurled down stones; but they made no attack when it came to close quarters, and, in the end, abandoned the position and fled.

The Greeks had no sooner got past this hill than they saw in front of them another hill, also occupied by the enemy. They decided to make an assault on this hill too, but Xenophon realized that, if they left the hill which they had just taken unguarded, the enemy might reoccupy it and make an attack on the baggage animals as they were going past. (The baggage train extended a long way, as it was going along a narrow road.) He therefore left on the hill the captains Cephisodorus the son of Cephiso-phon, an Athenian, and Archagoras, an exile from Argos, while he himself advanced with the rest upon the second hill and took it too by the same methods as before.

There was still a third hill left to deal with, and much the steepest of the three. It was the one that overlooked the guard who had been surprised at their fire during the night by the volunteers. However, when the Greeks got close to it, the natives gave up this hill without putting up a fight, a thing which surprised everyone and made them think that they had abandoned the hill through fear of being cut off and surrounded. Actually they had seen from the top what had happened further down the road and had all gone off to attack the rearguard.

Xenophon climbed to the summit with the youngest of his men, and ordered the rest to lead on slowly, so that the companies in the rear could join up with them, and he told them to halt under arms on level ground when they had gone a little way along the road. At this point Archagoras of Argos came running with the news that his men had been driven off the hill and that Cephisodorus and Amphicrates had been killed together with all the rest who had not managed to jump down from the rock and reach the rearguard. After achieving this success, the natives appeared on a ridge opposite the third hill. Xenophon spoke to them through an interpreter. He suggested a truce and asked them to hand over the dead. They replied that they would give back the bodies on condition that the Greeks did not burn their houses, and Xenophon agreed to this. However, while this conversation was going on and the rest of the army was going forward, all the natives in the district had rushed up: and when the Greeks began to come down from the hill and make their way towards the rest where they were standing by their arms, then, in great numbers and with terrific shouting, the enemy launched an attack. On reaching the summit of the hill from which Xenophon was descending, they began to roll down rocks. They broke one man's leg, and the man who was carrying Xenophon's shield ran away, taking the shield with him. Eurylochus of Lusia, however, a hoplite, ran up and held his shield in front of both of them during the retreat. The rest rejoined their comrades who were already in battle order.

The whole Greek army was now together again. They camped where they were and found a number of comfortable houses and plenty of food. There was a lot of wine, so much so that the people stored it in cellars which were plastered over the top. Xenophon and Chirisophus came to an arrangement with the enemy by which they got back the dead bodies and gave up their guide. For the dead they did, to the best of their ability, everything that is usually done at the burial of brave men. On the next day they set out without a guide, and the enemy fought back at them, and tried to stop their march by occupying any narrow passes there might be ahead of them. Whenever they got in the way of the vanguard, Xenophon led his men up into the mountains from the rear and made the road-block in front of the vanguard ineffectual by trying to get on to higher ground than those who were manning it; and whenever they made an attack on the rearguard, Chirisophus rendered this attempt to block the march ineffectual by altering direction and trying to get on to higher ground than those who were attempting it. So they were continually coming to each other's help and giving each other the most valuable support. There were times, too, when the natives gave a lot of trouble to the parties who had climbed up to higher ground, when they were on their way down again. The natives were quick on their feet, and so could get away even when they did not start running until we were right on top of them. Their only arms were bows and slings, and as bow-men they were very good. The bows they had were between four and five feet long and their arrows were of more than three feet. When they shot they put out the left foot and rested the bottom of the bow against it as they drew back the string. Their arrows went through shields and breast-plates. When the Greeks got hold of any, they fitted them with straps and used them as javelins. In this type of country the Cretans were extremely useful. Stratocles, a Cretan himself, was their commander.

8

The crossing into Armenia

They camped for this day in the villages overlooking the plain of the river Centrites, which is about two hundred feet across, and forms the boundary between Armenia and the country of the Carduchi. The Greeks rested here and were glad to see the plain. The river was more than half a mile distant from the Carduchian mountains. They felt very pleased, then, as they camped here, with plenty of provisions, and often talked over the hardships they had been through; for they had been fighting continually through all the seven days during which they had been going through the country of the Carduchi, and had suffered more than they had suffered in all their engagements with the King and with Tissaphernes. Consequently the thought that they had escaped from all this made them sleep well.

At dawn, however, they saw that on the other side of the river there were cavalry, ready for action, and prepared to prevent them crossing over: on the high ground above the cavalry were infantry formations to stop them getting into Armenia. These were Armenian, Mardian and Chaldaean mercenaries in the service of Orontas and Artouchas. The Chaldaeans were said to be a free nation and good fighting men. They were armed with long

wicker shields and spears. The high ground, on which
the infantry was formed up, was three or four hundred
feet away from the river. The only visible road led uphill
and looked as though it had been specially built.

It was at this point that the Greeks attempted to cross;
but, on making the attempt, they found that the water
rose above their breasts, and the river-bed was uneven,
covered with large slippery boulders. It was impossible
for them to hold their arms in the water and, if they
tried, the river swept them off their feet, while, if one
held one's arms above one's head, one was left with no
defence against the arrows and other missiles. They
therefore withdrew and camped where they were on the
bank of the river. They then saw that great numbers of
the Carduchi had got together under arms and were
occupying the position on the mountain where they had
been themselves on the previous night. At this point the
Greeks certainly felt very downhearted: they saw how
difficult the river was to cross, and they saw also the
troops ready to stop them crossing, and now the Carduchi waiting to set upon them from the rear if they
attempted it. So for that day and the following night
they stayed where they were, not knowing what to do.

Xenophon had a dream. He dreamed that he was
bound in fetters, but the fetters fell off of their own
accord, so that he was free and recovered the complete
use of his limbs. Just before dawn he went to Chirisophus
and told him that he felt confident that things would
be all right, and he related his dream. Chirisophus was
delighted, and at the first sign of dawn all the generals
assembled and offered a sacrifice. The appearance of the

victims was favourable from the very first. Then the generals and captains left the sacrifice and passed round the word to the troops to have their breakfast.

While Xenophon was having breakfast two young men came running up to him. Everyone knew that it was permissible to come to him whether he was in the middle of breakfast or supper, or to wake him from his sleep and talk to him, if they had anything to say which had a bearing on the fighting. These young men now told him that they had been collecting kindling for their fire, and had then seen on the other side of the river, on the rocks that went right down to the water, an old man and a woman and some girls storing away what looked like bundles of clothing in a hollow rock. On seeing this, they had come to the conclusion that this was a safe place to get across, as the ground there was inaccessible to the enemy's cavalry. So they had undressed and taken their daggers and gone across naked, expecting that they would have to swim. However, they went ahead and got to the other side without the water ever reaching up to the crutch. Once on the other side they made off with the clothing and came back again.

Xenophon at once poured a libation and gave directions for the young men to join in it and pray to the gods who had sent the dream and revealed the ford, that they should bring what remained to a happy fulfilment. As soon as he had made the libation he took the young men to Chirisophus and they told their story to him. Chirisophus, after hearing it, also made a libation, and, when the libations were over, they gave instructions for the soldiers to pack their belongings, while they

themselves called a meeting of the generals and discussed
the question of how to make the crossing as efficient as
possible, and how they could defeat the enemy in front
and at the same time suffer no losses from those in the
rear. They decided that Chirisophus should go first with
half the army, while the other half stayed behind with
Xenophon, and that the baggage animals and the general
crowd should go across between the two.

When things were in order, they set off, and the two
young men led the way, keeping the river on their left.
The way to the ford was a distance of less than half a mile
and, as they marched, the enemy's cavalry formations on
the other bank kept pace with them. On reaching the
bank of the river where the ford was, they grounded
arms, and then Chirisophus himself first put a ceremonial
wreath on his head, threw aside his cloak, and took up his
arms, telling the rest to follow his example. He ordered
the captains to lead their companies across in columns,
some on the left and others on the right of him. The soothsayers then cut the throats of the animals over the river,
and meanwhile the enemy were shooting arrows and
slinging. However, they were still out of range. The
appearance of the victims was pronounced favourable,
and then all the soldiers sang the paean and raised the
battle-cry, and all the women joined in the cry; for a
number of the soldiers had their mistresses with them in
the army.

Chirisophus and his men then went into the river.
Xenophon, with those of the rearguard who were quickest on their feet, ran back at full speed to the ford opposite
the road into the Armenian mountains. He was trying

to give the impression that he intended to make a cross-ing there and so cut off the cavalry on the river-bank. When the enemy saw that Chirisophus's men were getting across the river easily and that Xenophon's men were running back on their tracks, they became fright-ened of being cut off and fled at full speed in the direction, apparently, of the river crossing further up. However, on reaching the road, they turned uphill into the mountains. Lycius, who was in command of the cavalry formation, and Aeschines, who was in command of the formation of peltasts that accompanied Chirisophus, gave pursuit as soon as they saw the enemy in full retreat, and the soldiers shouted out to each other not to stay behind but to go on after them into the mountains. However, when Chirisophus had got across he did not pursue the cavalry, but immediately went up on to the high ground that went down to the river to attack the enemy who were up there. They, seeing their own cavalry in flight and hoplites moving up to attack them, abandoned the heights overlooking the river.

When Xenophon saw that things were going well on the other side, he made his way back as quickly as he could to that part of the army which had crossed, for there were also the Carduchi to think of, and they were evidently coming down into the plain with the intention of making an attack on the rear. Chirisophus was now holding the high ground, and Lycius, who with a few men had made an attempt at a pursuit, had captured some of their baggage animals, which they had aban-doned, and some fine clothing and some drinking cups as well. The Greek baggage train and the general crowd was actually engaged in crossing. Xenophon then brought his men round and halted them in battle order, facing the Carduchi. He ordered the captains to split up their companies into sections of twenty-five men and bring each section round into line on the left: the captains and the section commanders were then to advance towards the Carduchi while those in the rear were to halt facing the river.

As soon as the Carduchi saw that the troops in the rear of the general crowd were thinning out and that there appeared now to be only a few of them, they began to come on faster, chanting their songs as they came. Chirisophus, however, when his own position was secure, sent Xenophon the peltasts and slingers and archers, and told them to do what they were ordered. Xenophon saw them coming across, and sent a messenger to tell them not to cross, but to stay on the further bank: when his own men started to cross over, they were to go into the river on each side of them as though they intended to cross to the other side, the javelin-throwers with their weapons at the ready, and the archers with arrows fitted to their bowstrings; but they were not to go far into the river. The orders he gave to his own men were that, when they were within range of the enemy slingers and could hear the stones rattling on the shields, they were to sing the paean and charge: when the enemy ran away and the trumpeter sounded the attack from the river, the men in the rear were to wheel right and go first, and then they were all to run to the river and get across as fast as they could, each at the point opposite his own position, so as not to get in each other's way: the best man would be the one who got to the other side first.

The Carduchi saw that there were now not many left in the baggage train; for a number even of those who had been detailed to remain behind had gone over to see what was happening either to the animals or to their kit or to their mistresses. Consequently the Carduchi came on with confidence and began to sling stones and shoot arrows. The Greeks then sang the paean and advanced on them at the double. The natives could not stand up to them, since, though they were armed well enough for quick attacks and retreats in the mountains, when it came to standing up to close fighting they were insufficiently armed. At this point the trumpeter sounded the attack, and the enemy ran away all the faster, while the Greeks turned about and escaped across the river as quickly as they could. Some of the enemy saw what they were doing and ran back again to the river where they wounded a few men with their arrows; but the majority of them were obviously still running away even when the Greeks had got to the other side. The relieving party, in their desire to show off their courage, had gone into the water further than they should, and came back across the river after Xenophon's party. A few of these men too were wounded.

9

They sack the camp of Tiribazus

After crossing the river they formed up in order about midday and marched at least fifteen miles through Armenia, over country that was entirely flat, with gently sloping hills. Because of the wars between the Armenians and the Carduchi there were no villages near the river; but the one which they reached at the end of their march was a big one, containing a palace belonging to the satrap; most of the houses were built like fortresses and there were plenty of provisions. Then a two days' march of thirty miles took them past the sources of the river Tigris, and from here a three days' march of forty-five miles brought them to the Teleboas, a beautiful river, but not a large one. There were a number of villages near the river, and all this part is called Western Armenia. Its governor was Tiribazus who was a personal friend of the King, and when he was present no one else had the right to assist the King in mounting his horse. He now rode up to the Greeks with a cavalry escort and sent forward an interpreter to say that he would like to speak with their commanders. The generals thought it best to hear what he had to say and, going forward till they were within hearing distance, asked him what he wanted. He replied that he would like to come to terms by which he would undertake to do the Greeks no harm and they would undertake not to burn the houses, though they could take any supplies which they needed. The generals agreed to this and made a treaty on these terms.

After this came a three days' march of forty-five miles over level ground. Tiribazus with his force kept pace with them, with about a mile between the armies. In the course of the march they came to a palace with a number of villages, full of all kinds of supplies, in the vicinity. There was a heavy fall of snow in the night, while they were in camp here, and at dawn it was decided that troops with their officers should take up quarters separately in the villages. There were no enemies in sight, and it seemed a safe thing to do because of the quantity of snow that had fallen. In these quarters they had all kinds of good food – meat, corn, old wines with a delicious bouquet, raisins, and all sorts of vegetables. However, some of the soldiers who had wandered off some way from the camp reported that at night they had clearly seen a number of camp fires. The generals then decided that it was not safe for the troops to be in separate quarters, and that the whole army should be brought together again. Consequently they camped all together; and it looked also as though the weather was clearing up. However, while they were spending the night here, there was a tremendous fall of snow, so much of it that it covered over both the arms and the men lying on the ground. The baggage animals too were embedded in the snow. The soldiers felt very reluctant to get to their feet, as, when they were lying down, the snow which fell on them and did not slip off kept them warm. But when

Xenophon was tough enough to get up and, without putting his clothes on, to start splitting logs, someone else soon got up too and took over the job of splitting the wood from him. Then others also got up and lit fires and rubbed themselves down with ointment. A lot of ointment was found in this place and they used it instead of olive oil. It was made of hog's lard, sesame, bitter almonds and turpentine. A perfumed oil, too, made from the same ingredients, was found here.

After the snowstorm it was decided to take up separate quarters again under cover, and the soldiers went back with a lot of shouting and jubilation to the houses and the stores of food. The ones who, when they had left the houses, had acted like hooligans and burned them down, now had to pay for it by having uncomfortable quarters. The generals gave a detachment of men to Democrates of Temenus, and sent him out from here by night to the mountains where those who had been out of camp had said they had seen the fires. They chose him because he had already on previous occasions won the reputation for bringing in accurate information on subjects like this. When he said something was there, it was there; and when he said it wasn't, it wasn't. He now went out to the mountains and said that they had not seen any fires, but he returned with a prisoner who was armed with a Persian bow and quiver and a battle-axe like those which the Amazons carry. This prisoner was questioned as to where he came from, and said that he was a Persian and was going from Tiribazus's army to get provisions. They then asked him what was the size of the army and what was the purpose for which it had been mobilized. He replied that Tiribazus had under him his own force together with mercenary troops from the Chalybes and Taochi: his plan was to attack the Greeks, as they crossed the mountain, in a narrow pass through which went their only possible road.

When they heard this the generals decided to bring the army together again. They left a guard, with Sophaenetus the Stymphalian in command of those who stayed behind, and immediately set out, with the man who had been captured to show them the way. After they had crossed the mountains, the peltasts went forward, and, coming in sight of the enemy's camp, raised a shout and charged down on it without waiting for the hoplites. When the natives heard the noise, they did not stand their ground, but took to flight. In spite of this, some of them were killed and about twenty horses were captured, as was Tiribazus's own tent which contained some couches with silver legs and some drinking vessels; also some men who said that they were his bakers and cup-bearers.

As soon as the generals of the hoplites found out what had occurred, they decided to return to their camp as quickly as possible, in case an attack might be made on those who had been left behind. So they sounded the trumpets to call the men back, set off and got back to their camp on the same day.

10

Marching through the snow

Next day they decided that they ought to get away as fast as they could before the native army could re-assemble and occupy the pass. They packed their belongings at once and, taking a number of guides with them, set off through deep snow. On the same day they passed the height where Tiribazus had intended to attack them, and then pitched camp. From here a three days' march of forty-five miles through desert country brought them to the river Euphrates, which they crossed without getting wet beyond the navel. The source of the river was said to be not far from here.

Next came a three days' march of forty-five miles over level ground and through deep snow. The third day's march was a hard one, with a north wind blowing into their faces, cutting into absolutely everything like a knife and freezing people stiff. One of the soothsayers then proposed making a sacrifice to the wind and his suggestion was carried out. It was agreed by all that there was then a distinct falling off in the violence of the wind. The snow was six feet deep and many of the animals and the slaves perished in it, as did about thirty of the soldiers. They kept their fires going all night, as there was plenty of wood in the place where they camped, though those who came up late got no wood. The ones who had arrived before and had lit the fires would not let the latecomers approach their fire unless they gave them a share of their corn or any other foodstuff they had. So each shared with the other party what he had. When the fires were made, great pits were formed reaching down to the ground as the snow melted. This gave one a chance of measuring the depth of the snow.

The whole of the next day's march from here was through the snow, and a number of the soldiers suffered from bulimia. Xenophon, who, as he commanded the rearguard, came upon men who had collapsed, did not know what the disease was. However, someone who had had experience of it told him that it was a clear case of bulimia, and that if they had something to eat they would be able to stand up. So he went through the baggage train and distributed to the sufferers any edibles that he could find there, and also sent round those who were able to run with more supplies to them. As soon as they had had something to eat they stood up and went on marching.

On this march Chirisophus came to a village about nightfall, and found by the well some women and girls, who had come out of the village in front of the fortification to get water. They asked the Greeks who they were, and the interpreter replied in Persian and said they were on their way from the King to the satrap. The women answered that he was not there, and said that he was about three miles away. Since it was late, they went inside the fortification with the water-carriers to see the head-man of the village. So Chirisophus and as many of the troops as could camped there, but as for the rest of the soldiers, those who were unable to finish the march spent the night without food and without fires, and some died in the course of it. Some of the enemy too had formed themselves into bands and seized upon any baggage animals that could not make the journey, fighting among themselves for the animals. Soldiers who had lost the use of their eyes through snow-blindness or whose toes had dropped off from frostbite were left behind.

It was a relief to the eyes against snow-blindness if one held something black in front of the eyes while marching; and it was a help to the feet if one kept on the move and never stopped still, and took off one's shoes at night. If one slept with one's shoes on, the straps sank into the flesh and the soles of the shoes froze to the feet. This was the more likely to happen since, when their old shoes were worn out, they had made themselves shoes of undressed leather from the skins of oxen that had just been flayed. Some soldiers who were suffering from these kinds of complaints were left behind. They had seen a piece of ground that looked black because the snow had gone from it, and they imagined that the snow there had melted – as it actually had done – this being the effect of a fountain which was sending up vapour in a wooded hollow near by. The soldiers turned aside here, sat down, and refused to go any further.

As soon as Xenophon, who was with the rearguard, heard of this, he begged them, using every argument he could think of, not to get left behind. He told them that there were large numbers of the enemy, formed into bands, who were coming up in the rear, and in the end he got angry. They told him to kill them on the spot, for they could not possibly go on. Under the circumstances the best thing to do seemed to be to scare, if possible, the enemy who were coming up and so prevent them from falling upon the soldiers in their exhausted condition. By this time it was already dark, and the enemy were making a lot of noise as they advanced, quarrelling over the plunder which they had. Then the rearguard, since they had the use of their limbs, jumped up and charged the enemy at the double, while the sick men shouted as hard as they could and clashed their shields against their spears. The enemy were panic-stricken and threw themselves down through the snow into the wooded hollows, and not a sound was heard from them afterwards. Xenophon and his troops told the sick men that a detachment would come to help them on the next day, and he then proceeded with the march. However, before they had gone half a mile they came across some more soldiers resting by the road in the snow, all covered up, with no guard posted. Xenophon's men roused them up, but they said that the troops in front were not going forward. Xenophon then went past them and sent on the most able-bodied of the peltasts to find out what was holding them up. They reported back that the whole army was resting in this way; so Xenophon's men posted what guards they could, and also spent the night there, without a fire and without supper. When it was near daybreak Xenophon sent the youngest of his men back to the sick with instructions to make them get up and force them to march on. At this point Chirisophus sent a detachment from his troops in the village to see what was happening to the troops in the rear. Xenophon's men were glad to see them and handed over the sick to them to escort to the camp. They then went on themselves and, before they had marched two miles, got to the village where Chirisophus was camping. Now that they had joined forces again, it seemed safe for the troops to take up their quarters in the villages. Chirisophus stayed where he was, and the other officers drew lots for the villages which were in sight, and each went with his men to the one he got.

On this occasion Polycrates, an Athenian captain, asked leave to go on independently and, taking with him the men who were quickest on their feet, ran to the village which had been allotted to Xenophon and surprised all the villagers, with their head-man, inside the walls, together with seventeen colts which were kept there for tribute to the King, and the head-man's daughter, who had only been married nine days ago. Her husband had gone out to hunt hares and was not captured in the village.

The houses here were built underground; the entrances were like wells, but they broadened out lower down. There were tunnels dug in the ground for the animals, while the men went down by ladder. Inside the houses there were goats, sheep, cows and poultry with their young. All these animals were fed on food that was kept inside the houses. There was also wheat, barley, beans and barley-wine in great bowls. The actual grains of barley floated on top of the bowls, level with the brim, and in the bowls there were reeds of various sizes and without joints in them. When one was thirsty, one was meant to take a reed and suck the wine into one's mouth. It was a very strong wine, unless one mixed it with water, and, when one got used to it, it was a very pleasant drink.

Xenophon invited the chief of the village to have supper with him, and told him to be of good heart, as he was not going to be deprived of his children, and that, if he showed himself capable of doing the army a good turn until they reached another tribe, they would restock his house with provisions when they went away. He promised to co-operate and, to show his good intentions, told them of where some wine was buried. So for that night all the soldiers were quartered in the villages and slept there with all sorts of food around them, setting a guard over the head-man of the village and keeping a watchful eye on his children too.

On the next day Xenophon visited Chirisophus and took the head-man with him. Whenever he went past a village he turned into it to see those who were quartered there. Everywhere he found them feasting and merry-making, and they would invariably refuse to let him go before they had given him something for breakfast. In every single case they would have on the same table lamb, kid, pork, veal and chicken, and a number of loaves, both wheat and barley. When anyone wanted, as a gesture of friendship, to drink to a friend's health, he would drag him to a huge bowl, over which he would have to lean, sucking up the drink like an ox. They invited the head-man too to take what he liked, but he refused their invitations, only, if he caught sight of any of his relatives, he would take them along with him.

When they came to Chirisophus, they found his men also feasting, with wreaths of hay round their heads, and with Armenian boys in native dress waiting on them. They showed the boys what to do by signs, as though they were deaf mutes. After greeting each other, Chirisophus and Xenophon together interrogated the head-man through the interpreter who spoke Persian, and asked him what country this was. He replied that it was Armenia. Then they asked him for whom the horses were being kept, and he said that they were a tribute paid to the King. The next country, he said, was the land of the Chalybes, and he told them the way there.

Xenophon then went away and took the head-man back to his own people. He gave him back the horse (rather an old one) which he had taken, and told him to fatten it up and sacrifice it. This was because he had heard that it was sacred to the Sun and he was afraid that it might die, as the journey had done it no good. He took some of the colts himself, and gave one colt to each of the generals and captains. The horses in this part of the world were smaller than the Persian horses, but much more finely bred. The head-man told the Greeks to tie small bags round the feet of the horses and baggage animals whenever they made them go through snow, as, without these bags, they sank in up to their bellies.

11

They capture a pass by a manoeuvre

When the eighth day came, Xenophon handed over the head-man of the village to Chirisophus for a guide. He left behind all his family for him in the village, except for his son, who was just growing up. He gave the young man to Plisthenes of Amphipolis to look after, with the idea that, if the father was a reliable guide, he could take back his son too when he left them. They brought all the provisions they could into the head-man's house, and then packed their belongings and set out.

The head-man was not put under any restraint and led them on through the snow. When they had already marched for three days Chirisophus got angry with him for not having brought them to any villages. The man said that there were none in this part of the country. Chirisophus then struck him, but did not have him bound. As a result of this he ran away and escaped in the night, leaving his son behind. This affair – ill-treating the guide and then not taking adequate precautions – was the only occasion on the march when Chirisophus and Xenophon fell out. Plisthenes was devoted to the young man, took him home with him, and found him a most trusty companion.

They then marched for seven days, doing fifteen miles

a day, to the river Phasis, which was a hundred feet across. Next came a two days' march of thirty miles. At the pass which led down into the plain there were Chalybes, Taochi and Phasians to bar their way, and, when Chirisophus saw that the enemy was holding the pass, he came to a halt, keeping about three miles away from them, so as not to approach them while marching in column. He sent orders to the other officers to bring up their companies on his flank, so that the army should be in line. When the rearguard had got into position he called a meeting of the generals and captains, and spoke as follows: 'As you see, the enemy are holding the pass over the mountain. Now is the time to decide what is the best method of dealing with them. What I suggest is that we give orders to the troops to have a meal, and meanwhile decide whether it is best to cross the mountain today or tomorrow.'

'I think, on the other hand,' said Cleanor, 'that we should get ready for battle and make an attack, as soon as we have finished our meal. My reason is that, if we let this day go by, the enemy who are now watching us will gain confidence and if they do, others will probably join them in greater numbers.'

Xenophon spoke next, and said: 'This is my view. If we have to fight a battle, what we must see to is how we may fight with the greatest efficiency. But if we want to get across the mountain with the minimum of inconvenience, then, I think, what we must consider is how to ensure that our casualties in dead and wounded are as light as possible. The mountain, so far as we can see, extends for more than six miles, but except just for the part on our road, there is no evidence anywhere of men on guard against us. It would be a much better plan, then, for us to try to steal a bit of the undefended mountain from them when they are not looking, and to capture it from them, if we can, by taking the initiative, than to fight an action against a strong position and against troops who are waiting ready for us. It is much easier to march uphill without fighting than to march on the level when one has enemies on all sides; and one can see what is in front of one's feet better by night, when one is not fighting, than by day, if one is; and rough ground is easier for the feet, if one is not fighting as one marches, than level ground is, when there are weapons flying round one's head. I do not think that it is impossible for us to steal this ground from them. We can go by night, so as to be out of their observation; and we can keep far enough away from them to give them no chance of hearing us. And I would suggest that, if we make a feint at attacking here, we should find the rest of the mountain even less defended, as the enemy would be likely to stay here in a greater concentration. But I am not the person who ought to be talking about stealing. I gather that you Spartans, Chirisophus – I mean those of you who belong to the Peers – study how to steal from your earliest boyhood, and think that so far from it being a disgrace it is an actual distinction to steal anything that is not forbidden by law. And, so that you may become expert thieves and try to get away with what you steal, it is laid down by law that you get a beating if you are caught stealing. Here then is an excellent opportunity for you to give an exhibition of the way in which you were brought up, and to preserve us from blows, by seeing to it that we are not caught stealing our bit of mountain.'

'Well,' said Chirisophus, 'what I have gathered about you Athenians is that you are remarkably good at stealing public funds, even though it is a very risky business for whoever does so; and your best men are the greatest experts at it, that is if it is your best men who are considered the right people to be in the government. So here is a chance for you too to give an exhibition of the way in which you were brought up.'

'Then,' said Xenophon, 'I am prepared, as soon as we have had our meal, to take the rearguard and go to seize the position in the mountains. I have got guides already, as my light troops ambushed and made prisoners of a few of the natives who have been following behind to pick up what they could. I have also been informed by them that the mountains are not impassable: they provide pasture for goats and cattle. If, therefore, we once get hold of a part of the range, there will be a possible route for our baggage animals as well. I do not expect either that the enemy will stand their ground when they see that we are holding the heights and on a level with them, as they show no willingness at the moment to come down on to a level with us.'

'But why,' said Chirisophus, 'should you go and leave vacant the command of the rearguard? It would be better to send others, that is if some good soldiers do not come forward as volunteers.'

Then Aristonymus of Methydria, a commander of hoplites, and Aristeas of Chios, and Nicomachus of Oeta, commanders of light infantry, came forward, and it was agreed that they would light a number of fires as soon as they had seized the heights. When this was settled they had their meal, and afterwards Chirisophus led the army forward about a mile in the direction of the enemy, so as to give the impression that it was at this point that he intended to attack.

When they had had supper and it became dark, the troops detailed for the job set off and seized the mountain height, while the others rested where they were. As soon as the enemy realized that the heights had been occupied, they were on the look-out and kept a number of fires burning through the night. At daybreak Chirisophus offered sacrifices and then advanced on the road, while the troops who had seized the mountain ridge made an attack along the heights. Most of the enemy stood their ground at the pass, but part of them went to engage the troops on the heights. However, before the main bodies came to close quarters, the troops on the heights were in action and the Greeks were winning and driving the enemy back. At the same moment in the plain the Greek peltasts advanced at the double against the enemy's battle line, and Chirisophus with the hoplites followed at a quick march behind. However, when the enemy guarding the road saw that their troops higher up were being defeated, they took to flight. Not many of them were killed, but a very great number of shields were captured. The Greeks cut these shields up with their swords and so made them useless. When they reached the summit, they offered sacrifices and set up a trophy. Then they descended into the plain and came among villages full of plenty of good food.

12

The Greeks catch sight of the sea

Next came a five days' march of ninety miles into the country of the Taochi, and here provisions began to run short. The Taochi lived behind strong fortifications inside which they had all their provisions stored up. The Greeks arrived at one of these fortifications, which had no city or dwellings attached to it, but into which men and women and a lot of cattle had got together, and Chirisophus, as soon as he reached the place, launched an attack on it. When the first body of attackers became tired, another body of troops relieved them, and then another, since it was impossible to surround the place with the whole lot together, as there was precipitous ground all round it. On the arrival of Xenophon with the rearguard, both hoplites and peltasts, Chirisophus exclaimed: 'You have come where you are needed. This position must be taken. If we fail to do so, there are no supplies for the army.'

They then discussed the situation together, and, when Xenophon asked what it was that was stopping them from getting inside, Chirisophus said: 'This approach, which you see, is the only one there is. But when one tries to get in by that way, they roll down boulders from that rock which overhangs the position. Whoever gets caught by one, ends up like this.' And he pointed out some men who had had their legs and ribs broken.

'But,' said Xenophon, 'when they have used up their boulders, what is there to stop us getting inside? In front of us we see only these few men, and of these only two or three who are armed. And, as you can see yourself, the piece of ground where we are bound to be exposed to the stones, as we go over it, is about a hundred and fifty feet in length. Of this distance, about a hundred feet is covered with large pine trees spaced at intervals. If the men take shelter against their trunks, what damage could come to them either from the rolling stones or the stones flying through the air? All that is left is fifty feet, over which we must run when the stones cease coming at us.'

'But,' said Chirisophus, 'as soon as we begin to advance towards the wooded part, great numbers of stones are hurled down at us.'

'That,' said Xenophon, 'is just what we want. They will use up their stones all the quicker. Let us advance, then, to the point from which we shall not have far to run forward if we are to do so, and from which we can easily retreat if we want to.'

Then Chirisophus and Xenophon went forward, accompanied by one of the captains, Callimachus of Parrhasia, since on that day he held the position of chief officer among the captains of the rearguard. The other captains stayed behind in safety. Afterwards about seventy men reached the shelter of the trees, not in a body, but one by one, each man looking after himself as well as he could. Agasias of Stymphalus and Aristonymus of Methydria (also captains of the rearguard) with some others were standing by outside the trees, as it was not safe for more than one company to stand among them.

Callimachus had a good scheme. He kept running forward two or three paces from the tree under which he was sheltering and, when the stones came down on him, he nimbly drew back again. Each time he ran forward more than ten waggon loads of stones were used. Agasias saw that the whole army was watching what Callimachus was doing, and feared that he would not be the first man to get into the fortification; so, without calling in the help of Aristonymus, who was next to him, or of Eurylochus of Lusia, though both of them were friends of his, he went ahead by himself and got beyond everyone. When Callimachus saw that he was going past him he seized hold of him by his shield. Meantime Aristonymus of Methydria ran past them, and after him Eurylochus of Lusia. All of these men were keen rivals of each other in doing brave things, and so, struggling amongst themselves, they took the place. For, once they were inside, no more stones were thrown down from above.

Then it was certainly a terrible sight. The women threw their children down from the rocks and then threw themselves after them, and the men did the same. While this was going on Aeneas of Stymphalos, a captain, saw one of them, who was wearing a fine garment, running to throw himself down, and he caught hold of him in order to stop him; but the man dragged him with him and they both went hurtling down over the rocks and were killed. Consequently very few prisoners were taken, but there were great numbers of oxen and asses and sheep.

Then came a seven days' march of a hundred and fifty miles through the country of the Chalybes. These were the most warlike of all the tribes on their way, and they fought with the Greeks at close quarters. They had body-armour of linen, reaching down to the groin, and instead of skirts to their armour they wore thick twisted cords. They also wore greaves and helmets, and carried on their belts a knife of about the size of the Spartan dagger. With these knives they cut the throats of those whom they managed to overpower, and then would cut off their heads and carry them as they marched, singing and dancing whenever their enemies were likely to see them. They also carried a spear with one point, about twenty feet long. They used to stay inside their settlements, and then, when the Greeks had gone past, they would follow behind and were always ready for a fight. They had their houses in fortified positions, and had brought all their provisions inside the fortifications. Consequently the Greeks could take nothing from them, but lived on the supplies which they had seized from the Taochi.

The Greeks arrived next at the river Harpasus which was four hundred feet across. Then they marched through the territory of the Scytheni, a four days' march of sixty miles over level ground until they came to some villages, where they stayed for three days and renewed their stocks of provisions. Then a four days' march of sixty miles brought them to a large, prosperous and inhabited city, which was called Gymnias. The governor of the country sent the Greeks a guide from this city, with the idea that he should lead them through country

which was at war with his own people. When the guide
arrived, he said that in five days he would lead them to
a place from which they could see the sea; and he said
he was ready to be put to death if he failed to do so. So
he led the way, and, when they had crossed the border
into his enemies' country, he urged them to burn and
lay waste the land, thus making it clear that it was for
this purpose that he had come to them, and not because
of any goodwill to the Greeks.

They came to the mountain on the fifth day, the name
of the mountain being Thekes. When the men in front
reached the summit and caught sight of the sea there
was great shouting. Xenophon and the rearguard heard
it and thought that there were some more enemies
attacking in the front, since there were natives of the
country they had ravaged following them up behind,
and the rearguard had killed some of them and made
prisoners of others in an ambush, and captured about
twenty raw ox-hide shields, with the hair on. However,
when the shouting got louder and drew nearer, and
those who were constantly going forward started running towards the men in front who kept on shouting,
and the more there were of them the more shouting
there was, it looked then as though this was something
of considerable importance. So Xenophon mounted his
horse and, taking Lycus and the cavalry with him, rode
forward to give support, and, quite soon, they heard the
soldiers shouting out 'The sea! The sea!' and passing the
word down the column. Then certainly they all began
to run, the rearguard and all, and drove on the baggage
animals and the horses at full speed; and when they had

all got to the top, the soldiers, with tears in their eyes, embraced each other and their generals and captains. In a moment, at somebody or other's suggestion, they collected stones and made a great pile of them. On top they put a lot of raw ox-hides and staves and shields which they had captured. The guide himself cut the shields into pieces and urged the others to do so too. Afterwards the Greeks sent the guide back and gave him as presents from the common store a horse, and a silver cup and a Persian robe and ten darics. What he particularly wanted was the rings which the soldiers had and he got a number of these from them. He pointed out to them a village where they could camp, and showed them the road by which they had to go to the country of the Macrones. It was then evening and he went away, travelling by night.

13

They arrive at Trapezus

Then the Greeks did a three days' march of thirty miles through the country of the Macrones. On the first day they came to the river which forms the boundary between the territories of the Macrones and the Scytheni. On their right there was a defensive position which looked a very awkward one, and on the left there was another river, into which flowed the river that formed the boundary and which they had to cross. The banks of this river were covered with trees which, though not large, were growing thickly together. The Greeks cut the trees down when they came up to them, being anxious to get away from the place as quickly as they could. The Macrones, armed with shields and spears, and wearing hair tunics, were drawn up in battle order facing the crossing-place. They kept shouting to each other and hurling stones which fell harmlessly into the river as they failed to reach the other side.

At this point one of the peltasts came up to Xenophon. He said that he had been a slave in Athens and that he knew the language of these people. 'Indeed,' he went on, 'I think that this is my own country. If there is no objection, I should like to speak to them.'

'There is no objection at all,' Xenophon said. 'Speak to them and find out first of all who they are.'

He asked them this, and they replied that they were Macrones.

'Now ask them,' said Xenophon, 'why they are drawn up to oppose us and why they want to be our enemies.'

Their reply to this was: 'Because it is you who are invading our country.'

The generals then told the man to say, 'We are not coming with any hostile intentions. We have been making war on the King, and now we are going back to Greece and want to get to the sea.'

The Macrones asked whether the Greeks would give pledges that they meant what they said, and they replied that they would like both to give and to receive pledges. The Macrones then gave the Greeks a native spear, and the Greeks gave them a Greek one, as they said that these were the usual pledges. Both sides called on the gods to witness the agreement.

After exchanging pledges, the Macrones immediately helped the Greeks to cut down the trees and made a path for them in order to help them across. They mixed freely with the Greeks and provided them, as well as they could, with opportunities for buying food, and led them through their country for three days, until they brought them to the Colchian frontier. There were mountains here, which, though high, were not steep, and the Colchians were drawn up in battle order on the mountains. At first the Greeks formed up opposite them in line, with the intention of advancing on the mountain in that formation; but in the end the generals decided to meet and discuss what would be the best method of making the attack. Xenophon then expressed the opinion that it would be better to break up their present formation and to advance in columns. 'The line,' he said, 'will lose its cohesion directly, since we shall find some parts of the mountain easy going and other parts difficult. It will immediately make the men lose heart, if after being drawn up in line they see the line broken. Then, if we advance in a line many ranks deep, the enemy will have men on both our flanks, and can use them however they like. On the other hand, if we go forward in a line which is only a few ranks deep, there would be nothing surprising in our line being broken through, with masses of missiles and men all falling on us together. And if this takes place at any single point, the whole line will suffer for it. No, I propose that we should form up with the companies in column, spaced out so as to cover the ground in such a way that the companies on our extreme flanks are beyond the two wings of the enemy. By adopting this plan we shall out-flank the enemy's line, and, as we are advancing in columns, our bravest men will be the first to engage the enemy, and each officer will lead his company by the easiest route. As for the gaps between the columns, it will not be easy for the enemy to infiltrate, when there are companies both on his right and left; and it will not be easy to break through a company that is advancing in column. If any company is in difficulties, the nearest one will give support; and if at any point any one company can reach the summit, you can be sure that not a man among the enemy will stand his ground any longer.'

This plan was agreed upon, and they formed the companies into columns. Xenophon rode along from the right wing to the left and said to the soldiers: 'My friends, these people whom you see are the last obstacle which stops us from being where we have so long struggled to be. We ought, if we could, to eat them up alive.'

When everyone was in position and they had formed the companies, there were about eighty companies of hoplites, each company with roughly the strength of a hundred. They formed up the peltasts and the archers in three divisions, one beyond the left flank, one beyond the right, and one in the centre, each division being about six hundred strong. The order was then passed along for the soldiers to make their vows and to sing the paean. When this was done, they moved forward. Chirisophus and Xenophon, with the peltasts attached to them, were advancing outside the flanks of the enemy's line, and, when the enemy observed this, they ran to meet them, some to the right, some to the left, and lost cohesion, leaving a great gap in the centre of their line. The peltasts in the Arcadian division, commanded by Aeschines the Acarnanian, thinking that the enemy were running away, raised their battle-cry and advanced at the double. They were the first to get to the top of the mountain, and the Arcadian hoplites, commanded by Cleanor of Orchomenus, came after them. As soon as they charged, the enemy failed to stand their ground and ran away in a disorganized flight.

The Greeks ascended the mountain and camped in a number of villages which were well stocked with food. There was nothing remarkable about them, except that there were great numbers of beehives in these parts, and all the soldiers who ate the honey went off their heads and suffered from vomiting and diarrhoea and were unable to stand upright. Those who had only eaten a little behaved as though they were drunk, and those who had eaten a lot were like mad people. Some actually died. So there were numbers of them lying on the ground, as though after a defeat, and there was a general state of despondency. However, they were all alive on the next day, and came to themselves at about the same hour as they had eaten the honey the day before. On the third and fourth days they were able to get up, and felt just as if they had been taking medicine.

A two days' march of twenty-one miles from here brought them to the sea at Trapezus, an inhabited Greek city on the Euxine, a colony of Sinope in Colchian territory. They stayed here, camping in the Colchian villages, for about thirty days, and, using these villages as their base, they ravaged the Colchian country. The people of Trapezus provided the Greeks with facilities for buying food, and gave them presents of oxen and barley and wine. They also negotiated with them on behalf of the Colchians in the neighbourhood, particularly those who lived in the plain, and from them too there arrived presents of oxen.

Then the Greeks prepared to offer the sacrifice which they had vowed. Enough cattle had come in for them to be able to sacrifice to Zeus the Saviour and to Heracles, for safe guidance, and to make the offerings which they had vowed to the other gods. They also held athletic sports on the mountain where they were camping. They elected as organizer and president of the sports the Spartan Dracontius, who had been an exile from his home since boyhood because he had accidentally killed another boy with a dagger.

When the sacrifice was finished, they gave the hides to Dracontius and told him to lead the way to the place where he had set out the course. He then pointed to the ground where they were actually standing, and said: 'This hill is an excellent place for running, wherever one likes.'

'But how,' they asked, 'will people be able to wrestle on ground that is so hard and rough?' To which he replied: 'All the worse for the man who gets thrown.' Boys, mostly from among the prisoners, competed in the short-distance race, and more than sixty Cretans ran in the race over a long distance. There were also wrestling and boxing events, and all-in wrestling. It was a very fine performance, as there were many entrants for the events, and, with their comrades as spectators, the rivalry was keen. There was also a horse race in which they had to gallop down a steep bit of ground, turn round in the sea, and ride back to the altar. On the way down most of them had a thorough shaking, and on the way up, when the ground got very steep, the horses could scarcely get along at walking pace. So there was a lot of noise and laughter and people shouting out encouragements.